Disney Winnie the Pooh

It's Fun to Learn

The Big Bug Hunt

One day in the Hundred-Acre Wood, Tigger saw Christopher Robin holding a long list in his hand. “Watcha got there, Buddy Boy?” he asked.

“I have to find all these bugs for school, and I’m not sure where to look,” said Christopher Robin.

“Well,” said Tigger, “findin’ bugs is what tiggers do best. But firstest, I better findest some friends who can help! Be right back!”

Soon Tigger returned with Pooh, Piglet, Roo, and Owl. They carried all kinds of bug-spotting stuff.

"I've brought my honey pot in case I need a little smackerel," said Pooh.

"I've got my butterfly net and some treats," said Piglet.

"A boy on a bug hunt," said Owl. "My bug book will be just the thing!"

Roo handed out special headpieces for everyone to wear. "The bugs will think we look just like them!" he said excitedly.

Off they went on Christopher Robin's big bug hunt.

Looking up, Pooh saw a beehive. "You may want to cross honeybees off your list, Christopher Robin," said Pooh.

But Christopher Robin couldn't find his list anywhere.

"Don't worry," said Tigger. "We'll get all the bugs to come to us."

And together, everyone sang as they walked:

Yoo-hoo-hoo, hip-hip hooray! There're lots of bugs outside today.

We'll bounce along and give a shout: All bashful bugs, please come on out!

But their song didn't seem to work.

"I know what to do," said Owl, opening his book. "It says here that bugs can be found all over the woods. They like to perch on flowers and grass, hide under rocks, and crawl on tree trunks, branches, and leaves."

"Well," said Pooh. "That certainly gives us lots of places to look."

Suddenly Piglet swung his net in the air. "Shhh," he whispered. "We don't want to frighten the butterfly!"

The butterfly led Piglet and his friends to the pond.

"Ahem and ahoom, these bugs sure can zoom!" cried Tigger.

"Why, dragonflies are the fastest insects around," said Owl. "It's because they have two sets of wings. While I, of course, have only one."

Suddenly Piglet heard a curious sound. BOING-A, BOING-A, BOING-A!

"Listen," said Piglet nervously. "Do you hear something?"

"Hey!" cried Tigger. "Somebody around here is boinging, and it isn't me!"

"Oh, my word!" said Owl. "It's a grasshopper."

"Watch him hop!" cried Roo. "Hoppa-hoppa-hoppa!"

"Look!" said Tigger. "The poor little fella has to use his back legs for bouncin'. Since bouncin' is what tiggers do best, follow me, Buddy Boys!"

Everyone followed Tigger to the meadow.

"Let's look for more grasshoppers," said Roo.

But as they searched, Pooh accidentally left a little trail of honey everywhere he went.

"Hey, look at this insect!" cried Christopher Robin.

"Why, according to my book," said Owl, "you've discovered a banded woollybear caterpillar. I see he's the soft, fuzzy kind."

"Just like Piglet," said Pooh, causing his little friend to blush.

“It says on page three of my book,” Owl continued, “that a good place to see insects is in the garden. I’ll bet Rabbit has quite a nice collection.”

And sure enough, in Rabbit’s garden, Christopher Robin found ladybugs crawling on rosebushes—and on Eeyore.

"Don't suppose they've mistaken my nose for a rose, do you?" asked Eeyore.

"Whaddya know," said Tigger. "Bugs with polka dots! Maybe we'll find some stripedy ones next!"

When Tigger held the magnifying glass over a leafy plant, he found an incredible-looking striped insect. "Whaddya call that?"

"Well, I'll be," said Owl, shaking his head. "It's a red-banded leafhopper!"

"Hoo-hoo-hoo!" cried Tigger. "If I was a bug, I'd be an *orange-banded buddy-bouncer!*"

“Shhh! Listen,” interrupted Christopher Robin. “What’s that?”

“Those are field crickets chirping,” said Rabbit. “They make that sound by rubbing the edges of their wings together.”

“Sounds like they’re havin’ a wing-ding to me!” said Tigger, chuckling.

“Bother,” said Pooh, stopping to rest. “Looking for bugs is hard work.” Pooh shooed a bug out of the way so he wouldn’t sit on it.

“Stink, stink, stink!” said Pooh. “What do I smell?”

“I think you found a smelly old stink bug!” said Roo.

Just then, Tigger looked over at Rabbit's window. "That bug is settin' a trappin' for other insects!" he cried.

"You're watching a spider spin her web," Rabbit explained.

"Well," said Tigger, "even though spinnin' makes me dizzyin'...spinnin' is what tiggers do best! Yahooey!"

"Now here's *something* interesting," said Owl, holding up a leaf.

"Look at those tiny legs!" cried Tigger. "Why, there's a jillion, billion, ker-zillion of 'em!"

"I believe it's a millipede," said Owl.

"I'm tired just thinkin' about all the walkin' he must do," said Eeyore.

When everyone finally returned to where they had started, Christopher Robin spotted his list sticking out from under a rock.

"Here it is!" he cried, waving the list in the air. "Listen, everybody. It seems that we've found every kind of bug except for one—ants!"

“Oh, dear,” said Piglet. “I don’t think I can look anymore right now. Let’s have a snack and rest for a while.”

“Great idear, Piglet Ol’ Pal,” Tigger said. “We’ll have us a pickinick!”

But as soon as Piglet set out the blanket and food from his basket, Christopher Robin noticed an army of ants walking in Pooh's honey trail.

“They’re carrying crumbs back to the anthill where they live,” Owl explained.

“Well,” said Pooh thoughtfully. “Now we can send them a proper invitation to our picnic:

Honey, haycorns, carrot cake are what we love to eat.

Join us for a smackerel—if you want something sweet!”

“Oh, Pooh,” said Christopher Robin, laughing. “Silly ol’ bear!”

Fun to Learn Activity

Pooh and I had a wonderful time on my big bug hunt. Can you go back through the story and name all the different kinds of bugs we found? Do you remember where we found them?

Why not go on a little "bug hunt," too? See how many different kinds of bugs you can spot right in your very own backyard!